BABY-SITTER, GO HOME!

BAKERS' DOZEN

#4

BABY-SITTER, GO HOME!

Suzanne Weyn

A
LITTLE APPLE
PAPERBACK

SCHOLASTIC INC.
New York Toronto London Auckland Sydney

ISBN 0-590-43561-2

Copyright © 1992 by Daniel Weiss Associates, Inc., and Chardiet Unlimited, Inc. All rights reserved. Published by Scholastic Inc. APPLE PAPERBACKS is a registered trademark of Scholastic Inc.

12 11 10 9 8 7 6 5 4 3 2 1   2 3 4 5 6 7/9

Printed in the U.S.A.   28

First Scholastic printing, February 1992

To Karen Backstein —
thanks for all your
caring and guidance
on this series.

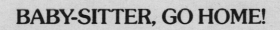

BABY-SITTER, GO HOME!

1

What's the Matter with Mom?

KENNY BAKER TUMBLED DOWN from a headstand onto the living room floor. "How long?" the eight-year-old asked his younger brother.

Five-year-old Jack Baker counted on his pudgy fingers as he sucked on an orange lollipop. "You've been downside up for thirteen-ten minutes."

"*Thirteen-ten!* You said you could count!" Kenny yelled. "There's no such number as thirteen-ten!"

1

"Uh-oh," said Jack. His orange lollipop fell from his mouth.

Seven-year-old Terry lay on the floor reading a comic. "Can you do this?" she asked Kenny, climbing to her feet. She did a perfect cartwheel. Her blonde curls bounced as she turned.

Before Kenny could try, a voice called out from the hallway. "Meet Jojo, super canine from the dog planet Barko!" Seven-year-old Howie Baker appeared in the doorway, a red cape tied around his neck. His thick glasses slid down his nose as he pointed dramatically down the hall.

Jojo did not appear.

Eight-year-old Collette Baker sat on the blue couch, threading a yellow ribbon into her thick, black braid. "Maybe he beamed up to some doghouse in the sky," she teased.

"Or maybe he's karate chopping Cat-woman," laughed Olivia Baker, looking up from the book she was reading. Her dark eyes shone with laughter behind her glasses. She was also eight.

"I *said,* 'Meet Jojo,' " Howie called again, this time louder.

"He won't keep his cape on!" someone called back.

Howie ran off to the kitchen. He soon returned, pulling Jojo, the Bakers' big, black Labrador retriever, by the collar. Behind Jojo was Kevin Baker, a six-year-old with lots of red curls and freckles.

Kevin wore a red cape just like Howie's. Jojo had a red cape on, too. But he wasn't at all happy about it.

"Those are my new red curtains!" shouted eight-year-old Hilary Baker, running down the stairs. Her brown hair flew around her shoulders as she ran.

Patty Baker — who was also eight — was right behind Hilary. "You mean *our* curtains, Hilary," she reminded her sister.

3

Hilary and Patty shared a room, but it had been Hilary's first. She still thought of it as hers alone.

Howie leapt up onto the couch. "You'll never get our power capes!" he shouted.

"Step on me and you die!" Collette warned as Howie ran across the couch.

"No! No!" Kevin laughed breathlessly from the floor. Patty had pounced on him and was wiggling her fingers in his face. "I'll really tickle you if you don't give the curtains back," she said, laughing, too.

A pretty teenager with long, curly brown hair came down the stairs. It was Christine, the oldest of the Baker kids. She crouched to zip up a backpack that sat in the front hall.

"Do you have money?" called Mrs. Baker, running down the stairs, her blonde ponytail bouncing behind her.

"You gave me money last night," Christine reminded her.

"That's right," said Mrs. Baker. "Call

me as soon as you get there. I still say this is too late in the season to go on a camping trip."

"Mother," said Christine. "I can't call you from the forest. There isn't a phone. And don't worry — Deirdre's family always goes camping this time of year. They have a camper and all this thermal stuff. I'll be fine."

"Mommy," came a small voice from the top of the stairs. It was three-year-old Dixie. Her pale skin was smeared with red lipstick. "I put on liplip like a big girl," she said proudly.

"Very pretty, sweetie," said Mrs. Baker, sighing slightly.

At that moment, a tall Asian boy of twelve came in the front door. He dribbled a basketball in front of him. "Mark, I borrowed your Walkman," Christine told him.

"Don't break it," he said as he passed on through to the kitchen.

A car horn honked. "That's Deirdre," said Christine.

Mrs. Baker stood at the door and watched Christine get into her friend's large white camper. Then she looked into the living room at her children.

Patty was tickling Kevin.

Hilary and Howie were tugging on either end of a red curtain.

Collette was whacking Howie with a sneaker.

Terry was teaching Olivia how to cartwheel.

Kenny was standing on his head.

And Jack was feeding Jojo his sticky lollipop.

One by one, the kids noticed their mother staring at them. One by one, they stopped what they were doing.

Mrs. Baker's face broke into a smile. Blowing them a kiss, she headed down the hall.

The Baker kids looked at one another, puzzled.

"Do you think Mom has been a little strange lately?" Collette asked after a moment.

"Definitely," agreed Hilary, letting go of the curtain. "Yesterday I found Dixie's shoes in the refrigerator. Mom left them there while she was getting some juice."

"And last night she ironed my ninja decal onto the seat of my pajamas," added Kevin.

"This morning she poured birdseed into Jojo's bowl," said Patty as she let Kevin get up.

"Maybe she just misses Dad," Terry suggested. Mr. Baker was away in Chicago at a special meeting of college teachers from all over the country.

"Maybe aliens have taken over her mind," said Howie.

"Aliens wouldn't do that," Olivia insisted. Olivia loved everything about outer space. She was sure that space aliens were very kindly creatures.

"I don't believe in aliens, but something weird is definitely going on," said Hilary. "Normal Mom would have said" — she took a deep breath and began to talk very fast — " 'Hilary and Howie, stop fighting. Collette, don't hit Howie. No basketball, cartwheels, or headstands in the house. Jack, don't give Jojo sweets. He'll get worms. All of you, go play outside. It's a beautiful Friday afternoon. Enjoy it.' "

"You're right," agreed Collette. "Something is really the matter with Mom."

2

The Chicken Pox
Warning

A WARM, YUMMY SMELL filled the Bakers' big kitchen.

"Ziti!" yelled Dixie excitedly. She jumped up and down in her seat. "Ziti! Ziti! Ziti!"

Mrs. Baker lifted one big sizzling pan of ziti from the oven. The cheese bubbled and popped on top of the pasta and tomato sauce. She set the pan down on a mat in the middle of the table.

Howie reached across the table and

stuck his fork into the pan. Mrs. Baker rapped the fork with her large serving spoon. "I'll serve, Howie," she said. "Just hold your horses."

"Neeee-iiiiii!" Howie whinnied like a horse.

"Very funny," Mrs. Baker said with a smile. She filled a plate and handed it to Collette. Collette handed it to Olivia. Olivia handed it to Terry. Terry handed it to Patty . . . and so on. Pretty soon, everyone had a plate of ziti.

Once the eating began, everyone talked at once.

"Juice, please," Dixie requested.

"Did you hear what Snoddy Goldleaf did on the bus today?" Hilary asked the group. "It was so disgusting!"

"Then we don't want to hear about it at the table," Mrs. Baker warned.

"Jack took my fork," Kevin complained.

"Get another," said Mrs. Baker.

Olivia nudged Patty. "Mom seems okay now," she whispered.

As Patty ate, she stole a quick peek at Mrs. Baker. "But she's not eating," Patty whispered back to Olivia.

Olivia saw that Patty was right. Mrs. Baker was pushing her ziti around on her plate.

Just then, Jojo barked. His head popped out from under the table. "Poor Jojo," Mark chuckled. "Nobody slips him food under the table on ziti nights."

"But everybody feeds him when we have spinach!" giggled Terry.

The kids laughed. But Mrs. Baker didn't. "Excuse me," she said, standing up. Quickly, she hurried out of the room.

The kids looked at one another. "Is she mad about the spinach?" asked Terry.

"I don't think so," said Mark. "She looked kind of pale."

"I don't like this," said Hilary nervously.

11

"She never should have adopted all you kids. It's too much for her."

"You're adopted, too," Collette pointed out.

"Yes, but I was the first. She should have realized one was enough," Hilary replied.

"One of *you* is too much," said Kenny. He wadded up his napkin and threw it at Hilary. It landed in Olivia's plate, splashing her with tomato sauce.

"Cut it out," cried Olivia, wiping the sauce from her glasses. "Stop fooling around. Something is wrong with Mom."

"Olivia's right," Mark told the group. "We have to be supergood — at least until we find out what's wrong."

At that moment, Mrs. Baker returned to the kitchen. Now the kids were on their best behavior. "Howard, please pass the juice pitcher," Hilary asked Howie.

Howie crossed his eyes at Hilary. He hated to be called Howard. Terry kicked him under the table. He jumped, but then he remembered that they were being good. "Certainly, Hilary, my darling sister, anything for you," he said, passing the pitcher.

For the rest of the meal, the kids continued to be extremely polite. Even Jojo sat off to the corner and didn't beg anyone to feed him a noodle.

"*What* is going on?" asked Mrs. Baker after Kenny politely offered Terry the last portion of ziti.

"Why, nothing at all, Mom," said Hilary. "You always tell us to be polite, don't you?"

Mrs. Baker sighed. "Of course, but . . . oh, well, I suppose I shouldn't complain. Whose night is it for dishes?"

"Patty's and Hilary's, but we'll all help," said Olivia. Everyone nodded in agreement.

Mrs. Baker wrinkled her brow. "Your father will never believe this," she muttered, looking very bewildered.

After Mrs. Baker left, the kids all pitched in to clean up. Even Jack and Dixie helped by sponging off the plastic tablecloth. As Jack stood on a chair and wiped, his pants began to slip down. "Hey, Jack, you're losing your drawers," said Collette, hiking up Jack's drooping pants. "What's this?" she asked, lifting a piece of paper that stuck out from his pants pocket.

"A note from my teacher," Jack replied. Collette looked at the note, it said:

Dear Parent:

Many of your child's classmates have come down with the chicken pox. This childhood disease is extremely contagious. Be on the lookout for signs of crankiness, lack of appetite, and fever in your child. These symptoms usually appear before the outbreak of spots.

Please return this with your sig-
nature by Wednesday.
    Thank you.
Veronica Thurm
Wild Falls Elementary
Kindergarten Class 1

"Jack, Wednesday was two days ago,"
said Collette.

"It was?" Jack said, running a pudgy
hand over his short, dark curls.

"Yep. You'd better get Mom to sign this
right now. Let's go find her," Collette
suggested, taking Jack by the hand.

"Hey, no running out on the dishes!"
yelled Hilary.

"Buzz off, Hilary," said Collette.

Jack and Collette searched all through
the house for Mrs. Baker. They went
upstairs to the second floor, then to the
third floor. "She's disappeared," said
Jack.

Collette and Jack went back downstairs.

"Anyone seen Mom?" Collette called into the kitchen.

"No," said Patty. The kitchen was clean, and the other kids had gone.

"Why are you doing homework in here?" Collette asked Patty.

"Hilary is practicing her ballet lessons in our room," Patty said, rolling her green eyes. "Did you look in the basement for Mom?"

"Good idea," said Collette. "Maybe she's doing wash."

Patty closed her notebook and got up. "I'll come with you," she said. "Chris told me there were some roller skates down there that might fit me."

The three kids opened the hallway door that led to the basement. *Chug-chug-chug* came the sound of the washing machine.

"Mom!" Collette called, walking down the steps.

There was no answer.

"Mommy!" shouted Jack.

Patty and Collette looked at one another. They were getting worried.

Walking into the middle of the basement, they looked around. "There she is!" said Jack. He pointed to a big, old, stuffed chair in the corner of the basement. Mrs. Baker was slumped over the side of the chair, and her eyes were shut!

3

Mrs. Baker's Big Surprise

"MOMMY!" JACK SHOUTED at the top of his lungs.

Mrs. Baker's eyes snapped open. For a moment, she looked dazed, as if she didn't recognize her own children. Then she sat up and smiled. "I guess I dozed off," she said.

"Man! You scared us!" Collette told her mother. "I thought you fainted or something."

Patty's eyes brimmed with tears. "Are you sick, Mom?" she blurted out. A tear rolled down her freckled cheek. "Are you going to die?"

"Oh, sweetheart, no," Mrs. Baker said. She got up from her chair, folded her arms around Patty, and hugged her tight. "I'm sorry you were scared. I'm fine."

After a moment, Mrs. Baker let Patty go. She looked at her three children. "Come on upstairs," she told them. "It's time I told you the truth. But I might as well tell everyone at once."

Collette, Jack, and Patty followed their mother to the first floor. "Family meeting!" Mrs. Baker shouted into the den where Olivia and Dixie were watching TV. "Family meeting!" she called up the stairs to Terry, Kenny, and Hilary. "Family meeting," she said, sticking her head into the living room where Mark, Howie, and Kevin were reading comic books.

The kids gathered in the kitchen. "There's something I want to tell all of you," she said.

"Is it terrible news?" asked Terry nervously.

"No. It's good news," Mrs. Baker said, smiling. She paused for a moment. "I'm going to have a baby."

"You're adopting *another* kid?" Hilary groaned.

"No," Mrs. Baker explained. "I'm pregnant. I'm having the baby myself."

For a moment there was silence. This *was* surprising news! The doctor had told Mrs. Baker that she'd never be able to have a baby. But obviously the doctor had been wrong.

"Wow! A baby," murmured Olivia quietly.

"Why do you need a baby?" asked Jack. "You have us."

"It was a surprise to us. We didn't know this baby would be coming," Mrs. Baker explained. "Don't you think you'd like to have a brother or sister?"

Jack thought a moment. "No. I don't think so," he said calmly. "Babies are noisy, and they spit up and stuff."

"Maybe you'll like the baby better when you really see him or her," suggested Mrs. Baker. "Babies can be a lot of fun."

"I want the baby. Can I have the baby?" asked Dixie excitedly. "My baby!"

"The baby will be your brother or sister, but it's different from having a doll," explained Mrs. Baker.

"When do we find out if it's a boy or a girl?" asked Kenny.

"I don't know," Mrs. Baker told him. "I'm not sure I want to know, either."

"How long will we have to wait?" Patty asked.

"Seven more months. The baby has been growing inside me for almost two months already. It takes nine months to make a baby."

"And two plus seven is nine," said Kevin, who was just learning to add.

"Gee, a baby!" sighed Collette. "I love babies."

"Is that why you weren't eating tonight?" Olivia asked.

Mrs. Baker smiled. "Sometimes being pregnant makes your stomach feel a little funny. I left the table because I felt sick. Most of the time I feel fine, though."

"Does the baby make you tired?" asked Patty. "Is that why you were sleeping in the basement?"

"Yes," Mrs. Baker replied. "Especially in the beginning. It's all perfectly normal, though."

"You call leaving sneakers in the refrigerator normal!" cried Hilary.

"I did *that*?" laughed Mrs. Baker.

"I found them," said Terry seriously.

"I guess I have been absentminded lately," Mrs. Baker admitted. "That's because I'm busy thinking about the baby, I suppose." Mrs. Baker looked at her children. Her face was bright with happiness.

Then a frown creased her brow. "Speaking of being absentminded, I forgot to ask why you were looking for me," she said to Collette and Patty.

Collette handed her Jack's note. "You have to sign this," she said. As Mrs. Baker read it, her face clouded over with worry.

"What's the matter?" asked Kenny.

"It says Jack has been exposed to chicken pox," she replied. "It could be very bad for the unborn baby if I were to catch chicken pox. Of course, if I had chicken pox already, I won't catch it from Jack."

"Don't you know if you had chicken pox?" Howie asked.

"Not really," said Mrs. Baker. "Remember, I was in an orphanage and then in different foster homes all my life. My medical records are scattered all over the place. And I don't recall if I had chicken

23

pox or not." Mrs. Baker headed out of the kitchen. "I'd better call Dr. Garner and see what she says."

"Who's Dr. Garner?" asked Olivia. "I never heard of her."

"She's a special baby doctor," said Mrs. Baker from the hallway. "I'm going to use my bedroom phone. I'll be right back."

The kids looked at one another. A new baby. They certainly hadn't expected that.

"Well, I guess you guys had better start packing," said Hilary.

"What do you mean?" asked Patty with alarm.

"Now that Mom is having her own kids, she'll probably be sending you all back to the children's shelter," Hilary stated matter-of-factly.

"If she sends us back, then she's sending you back, too," snapped Kenny.

"No, she's not," said Hilary, tossing her long, brown hair. "Mom and Dad knew *my* parents. They would feel too guilty to send me away."

"Just shut up, Hilary," said Collette. "You're scaring Jack and Dixie."

"Mom and Dad wouldn't send us away," agreed Olivia. "We're adopted. This isn't a foster home. This is a family."

"I don't want to go back to the shelter," said Patty in a small, frightened voice.

Mark put his hand on her shoulder. "Nobody's going anywhere," he told her. "Right now we should be more worried about Mom. I hope she doesn't get chicken pox."

In a few moments, Mrs. Baker returned to the kitchen. "Okay, kids. We've got a problem. Even though chicken pox usually isn't serious, Dr. Garner says I should get out of the house until she can track down my medical records. Just to be extra-safe."

"Can't you just stay away from Jack?" asked Mark.

Mrs. Baker shook her head. "Dr. Garner says any one of you kids could be coming down with chicken pox. She says it's all over the elementary school. I called your father in Chicago. He told me there's a storm, and he's not sure he can get a flight home."

"Maybe Grannie Baker can come over," Terry suggested.

"She left yesterday for her trip to Egypt," said Mrs. Baker. Grannie Baker was always traveling to interesting places.

"Don't worry, Mom," said Olivia. "We'll be okay here by ourselves."

"Yeah, Jojo and I can keep the little monsters in line," Mark assured his mother.

Mrs. Baker looked at her children. "No," she said after a moment. "I can't leave you in charge, Mark. You're just not old enough. If Chris were here . . . but I have no way to contact her. Of course, she will be back on Monday, but I'll need someone to stay with Dixie during school hours. Then again, your father may be back soon . . . but he teaches morning classes on Monday. . . ."

Suddenly she snapped her fingers and smiled. "I know what to do. I'll call a baby-sitting service."

Mrs. Baker took a fat, yellow phone book from inside a kitchen cabinet. She opened it and ran her finger down the page. "The Blue Bonnet Baby-sitting Service," she read. "That sounds nice."

The kids listened while Mrs. Baker spoke to someone on the other end of the phone. She told them her name and address. "I have twelve children," she said. "Yes, I am aware that that's a lot of children." Mrs. Baker rolled her eyes.

"Yes, I would need someone with a lot of experience," she said. "You do? Terrific! I'd need her as soon as possible. Great. In an hour? Perfect. Thanks. Goodbye."

"You got someone?" asked Mark.

"Yes. A Miss Peabody," Mrs. Baker answered. "She's one of their most reliable people. In fact, the woman there told me she wouldn't send anyone else to take care of twelve kids."

"Is the lady nice?" asked Dixie.

"I'm sure she is," said Mrs. Baker. "I'll be in town at the Wild Falls Inn. That's not far. And maybe your father will be able to get home soon."

While Mrs. Baker packed, the kids sat around the kitchen table talking about the new baby and what the baby-sitter might be like. "This will be great," Mark told them. "We'll be able to do whatever we want. We can go to sleep late, eat potato chips in bed, and have soda for breakfast."

"Really?" said Kevin happily.

"Sure," Mark said. "Baby-sitters don't care what you do. As long as you're still alive when your parents get home, they're happy."

In less than an hour, the doorbell rang.

"That must be her," said Olivia. "I hope she's nice."

"I want her to be pretty," said Dixie.

The kids hurried to the door. Mark pulled it open. A large woman wearing a brown cloth coat peered down at them. Her black and silver hair was pulled back into a tight bun. She had a long, slightly crooked nose, and thin, unsmiling lips.

"It's the wicked witch," Dixie cried, hiding behind Olivia.

The woman's dark eyes flashed at Dixie. Then, one at a time, she stared at each of the kids. "Hummph," she snorted unpleasantly. "I can see that I have my work cut out for me here."

4

Alone with Miss Peabody

MRS. BAKER STOOD at the front door. She wore her long blue jacket and carried a canvas overnight bag. She glanced nervously at her children. "You'll all be extra good for Miss Peabody, won't you?" she said. "Do you promise to do as she says?"

The kids looked at one another. They didn't want to promise to obey Miss Peabody. She looked too mean. But what else could they do?

30

"We promise," said Olivia. The rest of the kids nodded.

Suddenly, Dixie burst into tears, "Mommy, don't go!" she cried, throwing her arms around her mother's legs.

Mrs. Baker turned to Miss Peabody. "Maybe I shouldn't go," she said. "Dr. Garner will probably find out that I did have the chicken pox after all."

Miss Peabody placed her hands on Dixie's shoulders. Gently — but very firmly — she pulled Dixie away. "Nonsense," she said to Mrs. Baker. "Of course, you must go. You can't take chances with your health. Remember you are having a baby. It would be dangerous if you caught chicken pox and ran a high fever."

"Stay, Mommy," cried Jack. "If the chickenspooks come to my room, I'll tie them up and throw them in my closet."

Kevin thumped Jack on the shoulder. "Not chickenspooks. Chicken pox," he corrected him.

"That's what I said," Jack pouted, rubbing his shoulder. "Chickenspooks."

"Mommy, I'm scared!" cried Dixie. "Chickenspooks are coming."

Mrs. Baker knelt and spoke to Dixie. "There are no such things as chickenspooks, sweetie. The word is chicken pox and — "

"That's enough, children," Miss Peabody interrupted. "Your mother has to go. That's all there is to it."

"Yes, I suppose you're right," Mrs. Baker agreed, standing. "I'll be back — or Daddy will get here — as soon as possible. I love you all very much."

Miss Peabody opened the front door. "There won't be any problems," she said, guiding Mrs. Baker out the door.

Blowing her children a kiss, Mrs. Baker stepped outside. "All right," she said to Miss Peabody. "If you need me for anything, I gave you the number at the inn. It's taped to the — "

"We'll be fine," said Miss Peabody, shutting the door.

In the next moment, the kids heard the sound of Mrs. Baker driving away in the family's old van.

Miss Peabody turned and faced them. "Let us understand one another," she said sternly. "I am the law. What I say goes. If you don't agree with what I say — too bad. For as long as I am here, I am captain of this ship. Understood?"

The kids nodded.

"When do we get to have the potato chips in bed?" asked Jack.

"What potato chips?" snapped Miss Peabody. "What a revolting idea!"

"But Mark said — " Kevin began to object.

"Mark is not in charge," said Miss Peabody. She walked from the hall into the living room. Her big, black shoes squeaked slightly as she moved. "We'll get this room straightened up before bedtime," she said.

She ran her finger underneath the bottom of a picture frame. Her finger came up with dust on it. "Disgusting," she mumbled.

Just then, she spotted Jojo sleeping next to the couch. "What, may I ask, is that creature doing in the house?" she said, pointing.

"Sleeping," Howie replied. He turned to Kevin and whispered, "She's not too bright, is she?"

Miss Peabody glared at Howie. "I *know* he's sleeping," she said. "I meant, why is he in the house at all?"

"He lives here," said Collette.

Miss Peabody pulled Jojo up by his thick red collar. "Animals belong out of doors," she said.

Grrrrrrrrr, Jojo growled at Miss Peabody.

The woman jumped back. "Your mother allows this animal to wander, unleashed, through the house?" she cried.

"Dogs carry fleas and ticks! They shed, dirtying the furniture and fouling the air. And this dog is obviously vicious!"

"He's not vicious," said Mark, petting Jojo. "He's cool, aren't you, pal." Jojo nuzzled Mark's cheek.

"Cool or not — that dog is not sleeping here tonight. I want him outside," said Miss Peabody.

"It's cold!" cried Olivia.

"I'm not putting him out," said Mark defiantly.

Miss Peabody's eyes flashed. "Fine," she said, a frightening calmness in her voice. "In that case, I will have to leave. Your mother will be forced to return. If she becomes ill, you can blame yourself."

The kids watched and waited. What would Mark do?

His jaw jutted out angrily. But he didn't say anything. "Come on, Jojo," he said after a moment. "Let's go outside. You can sleep in the garage, I guess."

"He'll freeze to death!" shrieked Hilary. "It's frigid out there! We'll find him frozen stiff in the morning — icicles hanging from his blue nose."

"It's not that cold out there, and the animal is wearing a fur coat," Miss Peabody told Hilary. "There is no need for a hysterical display of sympathy. Cheap theatrics are the mark of a weak character."

Hilary stood with her mouth open. She wasn't exactly sure what Miss Peabody had said, but she knew she didn't like it.

"Come on, everybody," said Collette. "Let's all go get our blankets and make a warm bed for Jojo."

The kids began to move toward the stairs. Miss Peabody clapped her hands sharply. "Blankets will stay on the beds," she told them. "The young man can handle the dog. The rest of you will stay here and clean this living room. No doubt it is coated with dog hair. Tomorrow we will continue until the rest of this house is spotless. *Now take that filthy canine out of here!*"

Arf! Grrrrrrrr! Jojo barked at Miss Peabody as Mark led him out of the room.

Miss Peabody asked to be shown the closet that held the cleaning things. Then she gave everyone a job.

"Can I do this after my TV show?" asked Olivia as Miss Peabody handed her a dust rag. "It's called *Space Explorer*. It's all about a man and woman astronaut who go through space finding alien life-forms. I wait for it all week, and it's on right now."

"TV rots your mind," Miss Peabody stated, handing Olivia a can of spray polish.

"I'll go tape it for you," said Collette, laying down her dustpan. "Chris showed me how to tape stuff on the VCR."

"You will stay right here and clean," Miss Peabody insisted. "There will be no goofing off. This is a team effort." She

37

marched them all into the living room and stood — like a guard — as they worked.

After a while, the phone rang. Miss Peabody went and picked it up in the kitchen. "Oh, yes, Mrs. Baker," they heard her say. "Everything is just fine."

"Liar!" grumbled Hilary. "It's not fine, if you ask me."

Mark came in the front door and sat down on the living room couch. "Poor Jojo," he said. "He doesn't understand why he got kicked out. That woman is a witch."

"I knew she was a witch!" cried Dixie, burying her head in Patty's side.

"She's not a real witch," Patty said, smoothing Dixie's hair. "Mark meant that she's mean, that's all."

"The meanest," agreed Kenny.

Miss Peabody returned from the kitchen. "No chitchat," she said. "I want this room shipshape." The kids hurried back to their jobs. "It's time you two tiny children were in bed," she said to Jack and Dixie. "Come along."

"I don't want to go with her," Dixie whimpered.

Jack took her hand. "It's okay," he said bravely. "I'll protect you."

Their heads down, Jack and Dixie followed Miss Peabody up the stairs.

The minute Miss Peabody left, the kids stopped working. It was getting windy out. A shutter slammed against the window.

Arf! Arf! Arf! They heard Jojo barking from the garage.

"Jojo's scared," said Collette.

"I hope it doesn't thunder," said Terry. "You know how scared he gets in storms."

"It won't thunder," Mark assured her. "Most thunderstorms happen in the summer or early fall. I mean, it could happen. But it probably won't."

At that moment, a clap of thunder boomed outside.

Hoooooooowwwwwlllllllllll!

An ear-splitting howl rang through the air.

5

Space Ninjas to the Rescue

"Shhhhhhhhhhh," said Howie, pushing his glasses up on his nose.

"I can't help it," Kevin said. "I have the hiccups."

It was very late. The house was dark, and everyone was asleep. The only sounds were the ticking of the living room clock and the crack-boom of lightning and thunder.

Howie and Kevin were in the hallway, creeping slowly down the stairs. They were pretending to be space ninjas on a rescue mission.

"Hey!" someone whispered from the top of the stairs. It was Patty. "What are you guys doing?"

Howie put his finger to his lips. "Shhhhhhh!" he hissed.

"We're rescuing Jojo," Kevin told her.

Patty scampered down the stairs holding up her flannel nightgown in front of her. "I'm coming," she said.

"No girls on rescue missions," said Howie. "Go back to bed."

"Uh-uh," said Patty. "Pretend I'm Storm, the girl in the X-Men."

"The X-Men and space ninjas don't do missions together," said Howie with an impatient sigh.

"If you don't let me come, I'll wake Miss Peabody," Patty threatened.

"Welcome to the mission, Storm," Howie said, continuing down the stairs.

"Hiccup!" said Kevin.

"Shhhhhhhhhhhh!" said Patty and Howie.

They went to the front hall closet. Howie pulled out a big cardboard box filled with rubber boots and rain hats. "I can't see which boots are mine," said Patty, peering into the dark box.

"Just put on any ones," said Howie.

"Yugh," said Kevin, pulling a boot on his bare foot. "Rubber feels — hiccup — ooogy on your skin."

When their boots were on, Howie dug into the closet, looking for raincoats. He handed Kevin and Patty each a coat. "This must be Chris's," said Patty, pulling on the coat. "It's way too big."

"Come on," Howie said as he opened the front door. The three trudged through the pouring rain toward the garage.

Suddenly, a bolt of lightning cracked across the sky.

"Yow!" cried Kevin, throwing his arms around Howie.

For a moment, Kevin and Howie clung to one another. Patty covered her eyes with her hands. A clap of thunder crashed overhead.

Hooooowwwwlllllllllll, Jojo cried from the garage.

"Hey," said Kevin, looking up at Howie. "My hiccups are gone."

When they got to the garage, they pushed up the door. It took all three of them to raise it half way.

"I don't see him," whispered Patty.

"Jojo? Where are you?" Howie called softly into the dark garage.

Then they heard the low, whining sound of a dog crying. *Eu-eu-eu-eeeeeeee-uuuuuuuu-eu-eu.*

"He's under here," said Patty, squatting. Jojo had crawled under Grannie Baker's old broken pickup truck, which was stored in the Bakers' garage. "Come out, Jojo. It's us," Patty called to the dog.

Scratch. Scratch. Scratch. Jojo's nails scraped against the cement floor as he scurried out from under the car. *Arf! Arf!* he barked, happy to see the kids.

"Shhhhhhhhh," said Patty, Kevin, and Howie.

"Now we must safely return Jojo the Wonder Dog to his home planet, Barko," said Howie, slipping under the half-open garage door. Kevin, Patty, and Jojo followed him. Together, they ran back to the house. In minutes they were in the front hall. "We'll bring him up to our room," said Howie, wiping raindrops from his glasses. "That way Miss Pea-brain won't find him."

They threw their wet gear into the front hall. "Be very quiet," Patty told Jojo.

Arf! Jojo barked.

"Shhhhhhhhhhhh!" Howie and Kevin clamped their hands down on the dog's muzzle. They waited to see if Jojo had

45

awakened anyone. But everything was quiet, except for the steady ticking of the living room clock.

With Jojo in the middle, the kids crept up the stairs. Howie and Kevin shared a room on the second floor. They had to walk past their parents' room to get to it. That was the room Miss Peabody was using.

Slowly, quietly, they sneaked down the hall. "We are now passing the den of the evil Space Empress," Howie whispered as they neared Miss Peabody's room. "Proceed with extreme caution."

They were almost past the door when suddenly, it opened. Miss Peabody stood there in a long, gray flannel nightgown. Her wiry gray and black hair fell straight down to her shoulders. "What is going on?" she demanded.

Grrrrrrrrrr! Jojo growled, baring his teeth.

Miss Peabody jumped back. She shut the door all but a crack. "Call that dog off," she said fearfully through the narrow opening in the door.

"I don't know how to," Howie lied to Miss Peabody. "Once Jojo gets like this, there's no stopping him."

Arf! Arf! Grrrrrrrrrrr! Jojo continued.

The bedroom doors began to open. "What's the matter?" Collette asked, rubbing her eyes. Olivia and Terry walked sleepily out into the hall behind her.

"It's Jojo," said Patty, winking at her sisters. "He's out of control again."

"Out of control?" Terry mumbled. "Jojo never gets — "

A small shove from Collette stopped her. "Oh, yes," Terry stammered. "It's, it's terrible when he gets this way."

"He'll probably stand there and bark at you until you leave," Collette said to Miss Peabody, who was still huddled behind the door. "I don't know how you'll get past him. We may have to lower you out the window."

In a few minutes all the older kids were in the hallway. Jojo kept barking at Miss Peabody. "Who let that dog in?" asked Miss Peabody, opening the door a crack.

"He just walked in the front door," said Howie, hoping Miss Peabody wouldn't notice his wet hair. "When he wants to get somebody, nothing stops him."

Arf! Arf! Arf! Jojo continued.

"What a shame. He doesn't like you at all," said Mark.

"You'd better keep that door shut tight," added Hilary.

At that moment, a flash of lightning lit up the hallway. It was followed by a loud bang of thunder.

Jojo's tail drooped between his legs. He dropped to the floor and covered his head with his paws. *Eu-eu-euuuuueee-eu,* he whimpered pitifully.

Miss Peabody opened the door wide. Her eyes blazed with anger.

"So much for this fearsome creature!" she scoffed. "You, young man," she said, pointing at Mark. "Return this animal to the garage."

"But he's scared of the storm," Mark objected.

Miss Peabody squared her broad shoulders. "Do it now!" she bellowed.

"Come on, Jojo," said Mark, leading Jojo back down the stairs.

With a sharp clap of her hands, Miss Peabody sent the kids back to bed. "You three wet children," she called to Howie, Kevin, and Patty. "We will discuss your punishment tomorrow."

"Great," Patty mumbled glumly as she walked away behind Kevin and Howie. The boys went to their room at the end of the hall. Patty continued on up the stairs to her third-floor bedroom. Hilary was already in bed.

"Did you see the look on her face when Jojo was barking at her?" Hilary giggled. "What a scream!"

"Yeah, but now I'm going to get punished," Patty said as she dried her hair with a towel.

"Maybe not," said Hilary with a knowing little smile.

"What do you mean?" asked Patty.

A gentle knock sounded at the door. Hilary got up and opened it. In walked Collette, Olivia, Terry, Kenny, Mark, Howie, and Kevin. "Emergency family meeting," said Collette. "We have got to come up with a plan to get rid of Miss Peabody!"

6

Project POP

It was Saturday morning. Project POP was in effect. It stood for "Push Out Peabody."

Olivia, Collette, and Patty were still in the kitchen. They were cleaning up the breakfast dishes. It took a long time to scrape Miss Peabody's gooey oatmeal off the bowls. It had tasted terrible. And since Jojo was still stuck in the garage, he hadn't been under the table to eat it.

"My stomach is killing me," Olivia complained in a low voice as she stacked the dishwasher. "I hope this plan works."

"Me, too," agreed Collette, handing Olivia a cup.

"Me, three," whispered Patty. "You want to know what my punishment is? I can't play outside for the whole time Miss Peabody is here. Howie and Kevin can't, either."

"That's inhuman!" gasped Collette.

"Less chitchat and more work," Miss Peabody said. She sat at the kitchen table putting Dixie's wispy hair into a barrette.

"No! No! No! It hurts!" Dixie whimpered as she stood in front of Miss Peabody.

"You looked like a wild animal the other way," Miss Peabody insisted. "This is much better."

Suddenly, Hilary ran into the room waving an envelope. "A man just came to the door and delivered this for you," she said, handing Miss Peabody the envelope.

"He said it was unbelievably, incredibly important."

"I didn't hear the doorbell," Miss Peabody said as she tore open the envelope.

"Oh . . . I . . . um . . . just happened to open the door as he was reaching for the bell," replied Hilary. "It was the most hysterical coincidence."

Miss Peabody read the letter. "So, the agency wants me to leave here right away, do they?" she said, looking at Hilary.

"What a shame!" cried Collette. "And just when we were really getting to know you, too."

"They ask that I give them a call," Miss Peabody said, getting up from her chair.

Miss Peabody went to the kitchen phone and pressed some numbers. After a moment, she held the phone away from her ear. "This phone is broken," she said. "There's a strange clicking on the line."

"It does that all the time. It doesn't mean anything," said Olivia quickly.

Putting the phone back to her ear, Miss Peabody listened. "It *is* still ringing," she said.

"See?" said Olivia. "I'm sure someone will answer soon."

As Olivia spoke, Hilary was backing out of the kitchen. When she made it to the hallway, she bolted up the stairs to Christine's bedroom on the third floor.

She rushed into the bedroom. Kenny, Kevin, Mark, and Terry were on Chris's bed. Chris was the only Baker kid who had her own phone. The kids were giggling as Kenny played a tape recorder into the phone receiver. The recorder was playing the sound of a phone ringing. The kids had made the tape late last night. They had called Grannie Baker's number, knowing that she wasn't home.

"Answer the darn phone, idiot!" Hilary scolded Kenny.

Kenny snapped off the tape and

snatched up the phone. "Helllllllooooooooooooo," he answered in a high singsong voice. "Yes, this is the Blue Bonnet Babysitting Service. I'm the new phone answerer, Prunella. The regular person is out sick."

Terry covered her mouth to stop her giggles.

Kevin stuck his head under the pillow to cover his laughter.

By pressing the receiver button on Chris's phone, Kenny had cut off Miss Peabody's call to the real agency. Now he was pretending that *he* was the agency's secretary.

"Oh, yes, Miss Peabody!" said Kenny, his hazel eyes twinkling with laughter. "I'm so glad you called. Mrs. Baker phoned and said she will be returning home. You don't have to stay with those adorable Baker children any longer. . . . No, no. There is no need to wait for Mrs. Baker's return."

"Don't forget the President," Mark coached in a whisper.

"You won't want to wait when you hear what I am about to tell you," said Kenny dramatically. "The President of the United States needs someone to take care of his grandchildren. He asked for you. That's right. You. You are the only person who is trustworthy, loyal, true-blue, and perfect enough for the job."

Kenny listened as Miss Peabody spoke to him. The kids crowded around, trying to hear what she was saying. "Excellent, Miss Peabody," Kenny said after a moment. "We knew you wouldn't let your country down. Don't bother to stop by the agency. Just get on the first train to Washington. The President will be overjoyed to see you."

Kenny put down the phone. "Yes!" he cried. "She's packing!"

Kevin and Terry hugged one another happily.

Hilary skipped around the room. "No more Miss Peabody!"

Mark slapped Kenny on the back. "Good goin'," he praised his brother.

At that moment, there was a knock on the door.

Everyone froze.

With a small creak, the door was pushed open. Miss Peabody stood before them.

"Uh, hi, Miss Peabody," said Mark, sitting on top of the tape recorder. "What's up?"

"The sky, the moon, the sun," she replied without a smile.

"Oh, heh, heh," Mark laughed feebly. "I mean, what's happening?"

"A strange thing just happened," she said. "I spoke to my agency. And then I remembered something. The agency just started closing at eleven on weekends. I looked at my watch, and it's almost eleven-thirty."

"Maybe they kept it open just for you," said Hilary nervously.

"Maybe," Miss Peabody said stiffly. "But since they have my number here, I couldn't imagine why they didn't just call me."

"Totally weird," said Mark sympathetically.

"Then I remembered that there was a teenager in this house. Some misguided parents allow their teens to have phones in their rooms. Is there a phone in this room by any chance?"

Miss Peabody's eyes darted to the phone sitting on the bed. "I thought so," she snapped. "I am not so foolish as to fall for such an absurd prank. For one thing, the note you delivered to me had five spelling errors. The Blue Bonnet agency does not misspell words. Which one of you is Prunella?"

Kenny wiggled his fingers sheepishly. "Just a little joke," he said. "I can tell you have a great sense of humor."

But Miss Peabody wasn't laughing. "Lies, forgery, and deceit are not laughing matters," she told them. "I am putting you children under a group punishment. No TV for the remainder of my stay here. It is clear that your imaginations have been warped by too much TV."

Miss Peabody then turned on her heels and stormed down the hall. In the next moment, Olivia, Collette, Howie, and Patty appeared from the other end of the hall.

"Guess what," Terry said as they walked into the room.

"We know," grumbled Collette. "She already told us. No TV."

Jack and Dixie came to the doorway. Dixie's blonde wisps stood straight up in a hair clip. Jack's waves were plastered down with hair tonic. "Our hair hurts," said Jack miserably.

"Miss Peebleblody says we can't watch

cartoons," added Dixie. "Can she do that?"

"I'm afraid so," replied Patty.

It was as if even Jojo, out in the yard, knew how miserable they felt. He picked that moment to start barking.

"I want to call Mom and tell her that Miss Peabody is a horrible old prune face," said Collette. "But I suppose she has enough to worry about. We really shouldn't bother her."

"You're right," said Mark. "So we'll call Dad, instead."

7

Some Important Calls

"Okay, son, calm down," said Mr. Baker from the other end of the phone. "I'm trying to get home. I thought I had a flight, but it was canceled. There's another storm rolling in from the north."

"You've got to do something, Dad," said Mark. "She's driving us crazy."

"All right. Let me talk to Miss Peabody," Mr. Baker said with a sigh.

Mark held the phone to his chest. "Somebody get Miss Peabody," he said to the kids, who had gathered around him as he spoke on the kitchen phone. "Dad's going to talk to her."

"I'll get her," Hilary said. She ran out to the living room where Miss Peabody sat reading a book. "Miss Peabody," she called.

Miss Peabody looked up and took off her thick glasses.

"Our father would like to have a word with you, if you please," Hilary said in her most superior voice.

Miss Peabody squared her shoulders. "By all means," she replied in a voice that matched Hilary's. She got up and followed Hilary into the kitchen.

Mark handed her the phone. At first Miss Peabody did all the listening. "I'm sorry, Mr. Baker," she said after a minute or so. "I do not believe animals belong in the house. I have lived by this rule all my life and I cannot change now. Secondly, I must be free to punish the children as I see fit. You have hired me to keep order in this house, and I intend to do so."

Miss Peabody listened for a few more moments. Her face grew red with anger. "Then I will have no choice but to leave," she told Mr. Baker in an icy voice. "And let me advise you that it will not be easy to find another sitter at this late date."

"This doesn't sound too good," Collette whispered.

The other kids nodded grimly.

Mr. Baker spoke to Miss Peabody for a while longer. The red went out of her face, and she seemed less angry. "Well, all right," she said. "I suppose so. It's against my better judgment, but they are your children — and your blankets."

"All right!" whispered Kenny. "Dad set her straight."

Miss Peabody held out the phone. "Your father wishes to speak with you," she said.

Mark took the phone. "Can we bring Jojo in, Dad?"

"I'm afraid not," said Mr. Baker. "Jojo stays in the garage. I threatened to fire her, but you heard what she said. I can't risk your mother having to come home. It's too dangerous."

"I know that," said Mark glumly.

"I did talk Miss Peabody into allowing you to set Jojo up with blankets so he's comfortable. Dixie and Jack get to watch cartoons, *Sesame Street,* and *Mister Rogers.* The rest of the punishments stand, though."

"But, Dad — " Mark began.

"Sorry, Mark. There's nothing I can do. It's only for a little while longer."

"Okay," Mark agreed unhappily.

"By the way, how do you feel about the new baby coming?" Mr. Baker asked.

"Good, I guess," Mark replied. "Thirteen is a lot of kids, though."

Mr. Baker laughed. "It will be a real baker's dozen now."

"What do you mean?" Mark asked.

"A long time ago, if you bought a dozen rolls from a baker, he'd throw in a thirteenth roll for free. It was called a baker's dozen."

"I get it," said Mark. "Now that we'll have thirteen kids, we'll really be a baker's dozen. Cool."

Mr. Baker asked to speak to the rest of the kids. Since Miss Peabody was in the kitchen, they couldn't complain about her. "Come home soon, Daddy," Jack whispered into the phone.

"I'm trying," said Mr. Baker with a sigh.

"Are there chickenspooks where you are?" Dixie asked.

"I hope not," Mr. Baker chuckled.

After speaking to each of the kids, Mr. Baker said good-bye.

"Come on," said Collette. "Let's go bring Jojo some stuff to make him comfortable."

"You three stay," said Miss Peabody, pointing to Patty, Kevin, and Howie. "You are under house detention."

"Tell Jojo we said hi," Patty said sadly as the other kids left the kitchen.

In a few minutes everyone but Patty, Kevin, and Howie was in the garage. Earlier that morning, Mark had fed Jojo and let him out into the yard. Now the dog barked and jumped around happily when he saw the kids.

Collette, Olivia, and Terry piled blankets one on top of the other to make Jojo a nice, warm bed. As Olivia plumped the blankets, she saw Hilary plugging her electric rollers into a socket by the garage door. "What are you doing?" she asked. "This is no time to be setting your hair."

"I'm not setting my hair, silly," said Hilary. "These rollers get warm. We can put then in Jojo's bed. The cord reaches. See?"

"I don't believe it!" cried Collette. "You are donating your hair rollers! That is unusually unselfish of you, Hilary."

Hilary made a face at Collette. "I care

about Jojo just as much as you do," she snapped.

Olivia unplugged the rollers. "Nice idea, but you can't leave these plugged in all night. You might set the garage on fire."

"Picky, picky, picky," Hilary muttered as she gathered up the hair roller cord.

Mark came in carrying a boom-box. "I thought some music might make Jojo feel better," he explained.

"I wonder what kind of music he likes," said Kenny, who was lining up dog biscuits on a plate.

"Rock-and-roll, probably," said Mark as he tuned in a rock station.

"I read that animals, plants, and unborn babies like classical music best," Olivia told them.

"Do you mean the baby inside Mom can hear?" cried Terry.

Olivia nodded. "When it gets to be a certain size it can."

"Ooowww! Weird!" said Collette.

Jack and Dixie pulled a wagon into the garage. It was filled with stuffed toys. "We brought these to keep Jojo company," said Jack.

"That's sweet," Terry said. "He might chew them, though."

"That's all right," said Dixie. She looked out in the yard at Jojo and back at her toys. "Maybe he doesn't need Fluffy Bear," she said, lifting her favorite blue terry-cloth bear out of the wagon. "But he can play with the rest."

Jack arranged the stuffed toys around Jojo's bed. His big, dark eyes seemed heavy and troubled. "Will this show Jojo that we still love him?" he asked.

"Sure it will," said Collette.

"Really?" Jack asked. "Maybe he thinks we put him out because we don't love him. He might be very sad."

The kids looked out at Jojo. He was chasing a brown leaf that blew around the yard. "He seems okay now," Kenny observed.

"But maybe he's sad at night," Jack insisted. "I felt real sad last night. I missed Mommy and Daddy."

Dixie's lower lip began to tremble. "Me, too."

Collette put her arm around the two of them. "Hey, you guys. They'll be home soon."

"Let's see what else we can do to make Jojo happy," Olivia suggested.

The kids went back to the house to see what else they could find. As they neared the kitchen door, they heard the phone ring. "Oh, hello, Mrs. Baker," Miss Peabody answered.

"It's Mom!" cried Jack. "I bet she's coming home!"

8

Sad Jack

"MOMMY, PLEASE, PLEASE, *please* come home," Jack spoke into the phone. Tears brimmed in his dark eyes.

Poor Jack, thought Olivia, who was waiting for her turn to talk. *I've never seen him this unhappy. Hearing Mom's voice really set him off.*

"I have a tummy ache, Mommy!" Jack wailed. The tears now rolled down his plump cheeks. "I need you to come home."

Gently, Olivia took the phone from Jack. "Let me talk to Mom," she said. "Hi, Mom. It's Olivia."

"Sweetheart, would you be extra nice to Jack?" said Mrs. Baker. "I'm going to ask Miss Peabody to take his temperature and call me back if he's hot. But see if you can keep him busy so he won't miss me so much. Put on his favorite Mickey Mouse tapes."

"Okay," Olivia agreed. "He *has* seemed kind of droopy all day."

"I hope it's not the chicken pox," said Mrs. Baker. "Dr. Garner still can't track down my records. I lived in so many places as a child, I must have gone to at least fifteen different doctors. How are you doing?"

"I'm all right," said Olivia. She looked across the kitchen to where Miss Peabody was chopping cauliflower. "Miss Peabody is the worst," she whispered, cupping her hand over the phone.

"Try to be patient. One of us will be home soon," Mrs. Baker said. "Put Jack back on a minute, would you?"

Wiping his eyes, Jack took the phone. "Listen, sweetie," Mrs. Baker spoke soothingly. "Mommy is just in town at the Wild Falls Inn. I'm not far away at all. Daddy or I will be home very soon. You be a brave little boy."

"I want to come stay with you," Jack sniffled. "And Jojo, too. He wants to stay with you, too."

"No, baby, you can't," said Mrs. Baker.

"I want to," Jack insisted. "I'll be very good. Jojo will be good, too. Please, Mommy."

"I'm sorry, Jack. You just can't. Olivia is going to watch Mickey Mouse cartoons with you. Put Miss Peabody on the phone now, please."

"Miss Peabody," said Jack. "Mommy wants you."

Miss Peabody took the phone from him.

After she finished speaking to Mrs. Baker, she took Jack by the hand. "Please get me a thermometer," she said to Olivia.

The girls ran upstairs to the bathroom and found a thermometer. Jack sat on the couch while Miss Peabody put the thermometer under his tongue. After a few minutes, she took it out. "One hundred degrees," Miss Peabody read the thermometer. "Just a slight fever. I'm not bothering your mother for such a small thing."

"But Mom said to call her if he was sick," Olivia objected.

"A temperature of one hundred degrees is nothing for a child," said Miss Peabody. "I'll put him right to bed. Either he'll awaken with chicken pox in the morning, or he'll be just fine. And if he does have chicken pox, all the more reason *not* to summon your mother. Meanwhile, I'll keep watch on him. Now, to bed, young man."

"But it's daytime," said Jack. "I can't sleep in the day."

"Mom said to let him watch Mickey Mouse," said Olivia.

"This child doesn't need cartoons. He needs rest," Miss Peabody insisted. She took Jack's hand and led him down the hall to his room.

Olivia stood and watched them go. "Mommy lets Jojo stay with me when I'm sick," Olivia heard Jack say.

"Absolutely not," Miss Peabody replied.

Olivia sighed deeply. Things were not going well at all. She walked to the end of the hall and looked out the window. Mark and Kenny were playing Frisbee with Jojo in the front yard. Dixie was riding her tricycle up and down the driveway. Collette, Hilary, and Terry were pretending to be cheerleaders.

She went downstairs and found Patty, Kevin, and Howie in the living room. Patty lay upside down on the blue couch with her reddish-blonde hair hanging to the floor. "How about Lavender?" she asked. "If it's a girl, of course."

Howie had his legs draped over the side of the armchair. He pushed his thick glasses up his nose. "That's a totally putrid name," he said. "It's the name of a color. How about Igor?"

"That's good," Kevin agreed from his spot on the floor.

"Oh, gross!" laughed Olivia. "Are you trying to name the baby?"

"Yep," said Patty, pulling herself up.

Olivia sat on the coffee table. "Sally is my favorite name. I wish my name was Sally. The baby can have it, though."

"Don't tell me!" teased Howie. "That wouldn't be because it's the name of the first American woman astronaut, would it?"

"So what if it is?" sniffed Olivia. "That only makes it an even more special name."

"I wonder what it will be like to have a

little baby around here," said Patty.

"A pain," Howie said. "Babies just drool all over everything."

"Mom and Dad wouldn't really send us back, would they?" Kevin asked seriously. "I mean, when the new baby comes."

For a moment all of them were quiet. This was the worst thing they could imagine happening. "They can't send us back," said Howie. "We're adopted, remember. That means they're stuck with us. We're not foster kids anymore."

"Do you think they'd *want* to send us back?" asked Patty nervously. She had only been with the Bakers for three months. Her adoption was not yet final. The memory of the children's shelter was still very fresh in her mind.

"Look," said Olivia sensibly. "Nobody forced Mom and Dad to adopt us. They did it because they love us. So that's that."

"Yeah," said Howie, brightening. "And look on the good side. If they do send one of us back, maybe it will be Hilary."

Patty hit Howie with a pillow. "That's not nice," she laughed. "Hilary isn't *that* bad."

The rest of the day went slowly. Miss Peabody called them all inside for a big cleanup. "What a crummy way to spend a Saturday," Kenny muttered as he swept the floor.

"You children used a large part of your free time in a foolish prank," Miss Peabody reminded them. "Next time, use your time more wisely."

The evening went even more slowly. Miss Peabody made two big pans of cauliflower and tuna casserole. It stuck to the roofs of their mouths. Sticky, tasteless clumps of mushy cauliflower.

"I never tasted anything so disgusting in my life," Hilary mumbled, her mouth full of food.

Terry quietly spit her food into her napkin and stuck it under her plate. Then she stared down at the mountain of it that was still left. *I wish Jojo were here to eat this,* she thought unhappily.

Just as she had on the night before, Miss Peabody insisted they all go to bed by eight-thirty. She checked each room to make sure the lights were out. After she checked their room, Patty and Hilary turned their reading lamps back on and continued to read. They were usually allowed to stay up until ten on Saturday nights.

Outside, the wind tossed the trees. At about ten o'clock, Patty set aside her book and looked out into the dark, windy night. "At least it's not thundering," she said to Hilary.

But Hilary didn't answer. She was sleeping, her fashion magazine still on her lap. Her mouth was open, and she snored lightly.

Patty yawned and reached up to turn off her light. Then she remembered something she wanted to do. Hopping out of bed, she pulled on her flannel robe. She took a candy bar from her top drawer. Patty had been saving it for the weekend. But this evening she'd decided to leave it in Jack's room. It might cheer him up when he awoke in the morning.

Quietly Patty walked down the steps to the second floor. There was a light shining under the door of Miss Peabody's room. Holding her breath, Patty tiptoed past the room. She stopped in front of Jack's narrow room and gently pushed in the door. Patty didn't want to wake the sleeping boy.

But Jack wasn't in his bed!

Patty ran to the bathroom. He wasn't there. "Jack!" she called. "Jack!"

She ran to each bedroom and woke her brothers and sisters. "Have you seen Jack?" she asked.

No one had. Soon all the kids were out in the hall looking for Jack. They checked under the beds and in the closets.

"Maybe the chickenspooks got him," said Dixie, rubbing her sleepy eyes.

At that moment, Miss Peabody stepped out of her room. "What is going on *now*?" she demanded.

"Is Jack with you?" asked Collette.

"Why, no. Isn't he in bed?" Miss Peabody asked, panic in her voice.

"No, he's not!" shouted Hilary. "Jack has run away. And it's all your fault!"

9

The Night of
the Chickenspooks

"Jack!" Collette called out the front
door. Miss Peabody and the kids had
searched every inch of the house. He
wasn't inside.

"Hey," said Mark, coming up behind
Collette. "Maybe he's in the garage with
Jojo."

Collette's dark eyes lit up. "You're
right," she said. "That's *got* to be where
he is."

Holding their robes tightly, Collette and

Mark ran out into the night. The wind whipped Collette's long, black hair around her face. Together, she and Mark pushed up the heavy garage door.

Mark and Collette peered into the garage. The darkness made it hard to see. Groping along the wall, Mark found a light switch and turned it on.

Jojo was not in the bed they had made for him.

"Here, boy," Mark called.

Collette checked under the truck. He wasn't there.

For a moment, Collette and Mark stared at one another. "Oh, no!" cried Mark. "Jack must have run off somewhere with Jojo!"

They raced back to the house. All the kids were in the front hall putting their jackets on. Howie had found five flashlights in the closet and was handing them out. "Hurry up," Collette told her sisters and brothers. "Jack is definitely outside. He's taken Jojo with him."

Miss Peabody ran into the hall. Her wiry hair was unbrushed and loose. "Children, now stay calm. I want all of you to remain in the house. I will take care of this."

"No way," said Mark. "Our brother is out there, and we're going to find him."

Without waiting for her reply, the kids followed Mark out of the house. "Oh, very well," Miss Peabody muttered, running out into the yard behind them.

"Jack! Where are you!" the kids cried, sweeping the yard with their lights.

The only reply was the howling of the wind.

They searched the backyard. No luck. Suddenly, fat raindrops hit the kids in the face. "This is terrible!" cried Hilary. "Now he's lost in the rain."

"Jack! My Jack is lost!" cried Dixie who was clinging to Patty's hand. "He ran away from the witch!" Terrified, she began to wail at the top of her lungs.

"Hush, now," said Miss Peabody, picking up Dixie. "You stay with me. I don't want you getting lost, too."

"I won't stay with you!" Dixie screamed. "You're mean. Mean!"

"I'll hang on to her," said Patty.

Miss Peabody put Dixie down by Patty. "All right. I can't deal with tantrums now," she said.

"Do you think he'd go into the woods?" asked Olivia, nodding at the dark woods in the back of the Bakers' yard.

"What if he went down to the road?" said Collette. "It's so dark, and he's so little. A driver might not see him."

"I'll check the road," said Miss Peabody. "If he's not there, I'm going back to call the police. I want all of you to stay together. No one goes into those woods. Do you understand me?"

As she spoke, a clap of thunder rumbled in the distance.

Ow-ow-ow-woooooooooooooooooo!

"It's Jojo!" cried Kenny, pointing toward the woods. "Come on." With their flashlights held high, the kids charged into the woods. For a moment, there was a flash of distant lightning.

"Jojo!" they called.

Arf! Arf! Arf! came the reply.

"Jack!" Collette shouted.

"He's not answering!" gasped Patty. "What if he's hurt?"

As they ran through the woods, the wet leaves under their feet made them slip and slide. The *rap-rap-rap* of the rain hitting the dead leaves filled their ears. Suddenly, there was another bang of thunder.

Ow-ow-ow-ow-wooooooo! Jojo howled.

The next bolt of lightning lit the forest. "There's Jojo!" Mark shouted.

With the rest of the kids close behind, Mark charged down a steep hill. Jojo was there, standing up with his paws against a fallen tree. *Arf! Arf!* he barked urgently.

"Where's Jack?" Mark asked Jojo.

"I'm here," came a small voice by the fallen tree. There sat Jack, shivering. His knees were pulled up tightly to his chest. His damp hair clung to his forehead. Tears streamed down his pudgy cheeks.

Mark took off his robe and knelt beside Jack. "It's okay, now," he said, wrapping his robe around his brother. "We're here."

Just then, Miss Peabody came stumbling through the woods. "Everyone back to the house!" she shrieked. "This instant!"

"We found him!" Olivia called to Miss Peabody. By now all the kids had gathered around Jack.

Miss Peabody quickly caught up with them. "Oh, good heavens," she cried, placing her hand on Jack's forehead. "He's burning with fever."

"But, I'm so cold," said Jack, his teeth chattering.

"Yes, you have chills," said Miss Peabody. "A very high fever can sometimes make you feel cold and then hot. Why are you sitting? Have you hurt your legs?"

"They feel all wobbly," Jack told her.

"I imagine you do feel dizzy," Miss Peabody said, scooping Jack up into her arms.

Grrrrrrrrrrr! Jojo growled at Miss Peabody.

Mark patted the wet dog. "It's okay, boy. She won't hurt him."

"Come children. Home. Home, immediately," Miss Peabody commanded as she rushed back to the house.

In no time, Jack was dried off and in his bed. Miss Peabody checked Jack's belly. Ten small red dots stood out like mosquito bites. "Does he have chicken pox?" asked Hilary, who stood with the other kids in the doorway.

"He most certainly does," Miss Peabody replied. She had called the doctor. He had confirmed that Jack had all the symptoms of chicken pox.

The doctor told Miss Peabody how to care for Jack. "We want to make sure he doesn't get something worse, like pneumonia. Bring him to the hospital if his fever goes any higher," he'd said.

Miss Peabody had done as the doctor ordered. Luckily, Jack's fever seemed to be going down.

"The chickenspooks got me," Jack said weakly.

"You scared us silly," Collette said to him.

Jack sniffled. "I just wanted to find Mommy. I was bringing Jojo to her, too. He was scared in the garage."

"That's enough talking," said Miss Peabody, laying a cool cloth on Jack's forehead. "Now, shoo, all of you. I don't need you annoying me while I tend to this child."

Hilary shut the door and let it slam just a little bit. "The nerve of that old hag," she huffed. "She forces Jack out into the storm. He almost dies. *We* have to go out and find him — and then she tells us to shoo!"

At that moment, Jojo shook the water from his fur, spraying the kids. "Ohhh, Jojo," moaned Collette. "Let's go dry you off."

Suddenly, the bedroom door opened. Miss Peabody clapped her hands sharply. "The situation is under control," she announced. "I want everyone to change pajamas and get to bed." With that, she took Jojo by the collar and led him down the stairs. Jojo seemed worn out by his adventure. He didn't even bark at Miss Peabody.

"How can she put him out after everything that's happened?" cried Patty. "If it wasn't for Jojo, who knows what might have happened to Jack!"

"She can forget it," said Mark angrily. "I'm telling that witch off, and then I'm bringing Jojo inside. Who cares if she leaves! We can take care of ourselves."

"That's right!" agreed Collette. "She's pushed us around long enough."

"Mom and Dad will just have to understand," added Kenny.

"Let's tell her to go pack her things right now," Olivia said.

"Yeah! Scram! Beat it! Get out of here!" shouted Dixie in her best Oscar the Grouch voice.

"Come on," said Howie. "Let's beam the Evil Empress back to her home planet."

Feeling bold and angry, the kids stormed down the hall. It was time to let Miss Peabody know what they thought of her!

10

Home Again

"WHO GETS TO TELL her off first?" asked Kenny as the kids walked toward the kitchen.

"Me. I'm the oldest one here," Mark said. Patting down his damp hair, he took a deep breath and prepared to face Miss Peabody. He was the first to arrive at the kitchen entrance. But when he got there, he stepped back into the hallway.

"What are you? Chicken?" said Hilary,

stepping forward. "I'll go tell her off, then."

Mark grabbed her arm and pulled her back from the doorway. "Look," he said quietly.

"Wow!" Hilary gasped. The other kids crowded around and peeked into the doorway. Miss Peabody sat on a kitchen chair holding a large bath towel. She was drying off Jojo.

And she was crying.

"When I think of what might have happened to that child . . ." she said to Jojo in a choked voice. "You did a better job of taking care of him than I did. Imagine that!"

Dixie picked that moment to sneeze. Miss Peabody looked up and saw the kids watching her. Quickly, she brushed the tears from her eyes. "Yes, children?" she said.

The kids looked at one another. Somehow they didn't feel like yelling at Miss

Peabody anymore. She seemed to feel bad enough already."We wanted to ask if Jojo could stay inside tonight," Mark spoke up.

Miss Peabody looked down at the dog. "An animal in the house is most unsanitary," she said. Once again, she seemed to be her old, stern self. "Especially with a sick child . . ." Suddenly her voice trailed off. The hard lines of her face softened a bit as she looked down at Jojo. "Perhaps just for tonight," she relented. "I suppose he's earned that privilege."

"We told you he was a good dog," said Collette.

"Yes, you did," Miss Peabody admitted. A small smile formed on her thin lips. In a moment, it was gone. "Now, off to bed," she ordered, clapping her hands sharply.

Dixie yawned. "Is Jack safe from the chickenspooks now?"

"Yes," said Miss Peabody guiding her up the stairs along with the others. "The chickenspooks are all gone."

The next morning, Terry sat up in her top bunk. She sniffed the air. "Pancakes!" she cried.

"You're right," said Collette, in the bunk below her. "Let's go."

"Wait for me," said Olivia, grabbing her glasses from the nightstand.

As the three girls ran down the stairs, they met Howie and Kevin running back up. "You have to get dressed," said Howie, racing toward his room. "Miss Peabody says pajamas are not proper attire for Sunday morning breakfast."

"Oh, brother," sighed Collette.

"But she made real blueberry pancakes," said Patty, who was also returning to her room to get dressed.

"And bacon," added Hilary, coming up the stairs.

As soon as they were dressed, the kids returned to the kitchen. Miss Peabody had set two tall stacks of blueberry pancakes at either end of the table. A platter of bacon sat in the middle by three pitchers of orange juice.

"Let me at 'em," cried Kenny hungrily.

"Control yourself, young man," Miss Peabody said tartly. "We are not wild animals. I want everyone seated before I will serve a single pancake."

Eager to eat, the kids took their seats. "Look at Jojo," Patty whispered to Kenny. The dog was happily lapping up a pancake from his bowl.

"You let Jojo eat ahead of everyone," Kenny teased.

A pink blush of embarrassment crossed Miss Peabody's face. "Jojo and I have been getting to know one another better," she stated.

When the pancakes were served, Miss Peabody gave them all permission to eat. "I will return," she told them. "I am taking this plate up to Jack — who is now abloom with chicken pox spots."

"Dig in!" cried Howie as Miss Peabody left the room. The pancakes were as delicious as they smelled.

"Good thing she didn't put cauliflower in them," giggled Terry.

"Yeah, she should stick to cooking pancakes," agreed Mark.

At that moment, they heard the front door open. In a moment, Mrs. Baker walked into the kitchen. "My, my," she said, smiling brightly. "Look at these lovely children eating such a nice breakfast on this Sunday morning."

"Mom!" the kids shouted, jumping up from their seats. They crowded around Mrs. Baker, hugging and kissing her.

"Dr. Garner found my records and called this morning," Mrs. Baker said. "I *did* have chicken pox as it turns out. I can't catch them twice."

"Jack has spots on him, Mommy," Dixie informed Mrs. Baker.

"Oh, dear," said Mrs. Baker. "I'd better go see him."

Suddenly the back door flew open. It was Mr. Baker. His coat was crumpled, and his wispy blond hair stood out at odd angles. There were dark circles under his eyes. "I'm home. I stayed up all night at the airport, but I did it. I got a flight home," he announced proudly.

He looked at his kids, then noticed his wife. "What are you doing here?" he asked.

Mrs. Baker laughed and hugged him. "I just got here. Dr. Garner found my records. I had the chicken pox as a child."

"Great!" said Mr. Baker through a wide yawn. "How do you feel?"

"Fine. And happy to be home," said Mrs. Baker. "But Jack did get the chicken pox. Why don't you go say hello to him and then get some sleep?"

"Mmmmmmmmm. Okay," said Mr.

Baker, seeming to fall asleep as he spoke. "See you later, kids."

"Later, Dad," laughed Mark.

Mrs. Baker looked around the kitchen. "The house looks great, so neat and clean," she commented. "And you kids are all dressed. You're usually still hanging around in your pajamas early Sunday morning."

"Miss Peabody made us," Olivia told her.

"It's too bad you dislike her so much," said Mrs. Baker. "It looks to me like she's done a great job. I was thinking of hiring someone to help me a few days a week."

"She wasn't *that* bad," said Collette. "We were kind of starting to get used to her."

"Why, thank you," said Miss Peabody, stepping into the kitchen. "I was beginning to get used to all of you, as well."

"Would you be interested in helping me with the children and the house for three days a week?" Mrs. Baker asked her.

"I don't think your children would be very happy with that," said Miss Peabody, taking off her apron.

"Would you let Jojo in the house?" asked Mark.

"Well," said Miss Peabody. "I suppose I would."

"Would we be punished a lot?" Patty asked.

"If your mother were home, that would be up to her," Miss Peabody replied.

"It's okay by me," said Howie.

"Me, too," added Kevin.

All the kids agreed that Miss Peabody should come to help out their mother. "Then I will see you all in a few days. Right now I think I will go home and sleep for a good long time," she said, nodding at the family.

Mrs. Baker followed her out of the kitchen.

The kids sat and finished their break-fast. "It's great having things back to nor-mal," Patty said to Hilary.

As she spoke, a blueberry pancake sailed through the air past their noses. Another sailed over their heads.

"Howard! Grow up!" Hilary shouted at Howie, who had thrown the pancakes.

"Don't blame me," Howie replied, standing on his seat. "We're under attack from flying saucers. Run for your lives!"

"Yep," Patty laughed. "Things are def-initely back to normal."

12 times the fun with...

BAKERS' DOZEN

Great New Series!

by Suzanne Weyn

❏ NL43559-0 **#1 Make Room for Patty** $2.75

Eight-year-old Patty Conners has wanted a home and a loving family ever since her mother died three years ago. She gets her wish when the Bakers adopt her. But will one of her new sisters spoil it all?

❏ NL43560-4 **#2 Hilary and the Rich Girl** $2.75

Hilary's new classmate Alice has everything — a big house, beautiful dresses, and great toys. Now Hilary wants to be her friend — at any cost!

❏ NL43562-0 **#3 Collette's Magic Star** $2.75

Kenny has a terrible accident and is going blind. He needs an operation but there's no promise it will cure him. Can Collette and her magic star help Kenny see again?

Watch for new titles every three months!

Available wherever you buy books, or use this order form.

LITTLE 🍎 APPLE®

BABY-SITTERS

Little Sister™

by Ann M. Martin, author of *The Baby-sitters Club*

This little sister has a lot of big ideas! But when Karen puts her plans into action, they sometimes get all mixed up!

☐	MQ44300-3	#1	Karen's Witch	$2.75
☐	MQ44259-7	#2	Karen's Roller Skates	$2.75
☐	MQ44299-6	#3	Karen's Worst Day	$2.75
☐	MQ44264-3	#4	Karen's Kittycat Club	$2.75
☐	MQ44258-9	#5	Karen's School Picture	$2.75
☐	MQ44298-8	#6	Karen's Little Sister	$2.75
☐	MQ44257-0	#7	Karen's Birthday	$2.75
☐	MQ42670-2	#8	Karen's Haircut	$2.75
☐	MQ43652-X	#9	Karen's Sleepover	$2.75
☐	MQ43651-1	#10	Karen's Grandmothers	$2.50
☐	MQ43650-3	#11	Karen's Prize	$2.75
☐	MQ43649-X	#12	Karen's Ghost	$2.75
☐	MQ43648-1	#13	Karen's Surprise	$2.75
☐	MQ43646-5	#14	Karen's New Year	$2.75
☐	MQ43645-7	#15	Karen's in Love	$2.75
☐	MQ43644-9	#16	Karen's Goldfish	$2.75
☐	MQ43643-0	#17	Karen's Brothers	$2.75
☐	MQ43642-2	#18	Karen's Home-Run	$2.75
☐	MQ43641-4	#10	Karen's Good-Bye	$2.75
☐	MQ44823-4	#20	Karen's Carnival	$2.75
☐	MQ44824-2	#21	Karen's New Teacher	$2.75
☐	MQ44833-1	#22	Karen's Little Witch	$2.75
☐	MQ44832-3	#23	Karen's Doll	$2.75
☐	MQ44859-5	#2	Karen's School Trip	$2.75
☐	MQ44831-5	#25	Karen's Pen Pal	$2.75
☐	MQ43647-3		Karen's Wish Baby-sitters Little Sister Super Special #1	$2.95
☐	MQ44834-0		Karen's Plane Trip Baby-sitters Little Sister Super Special #2	$2.95
☐	MQ44834-0		Karen's Mystery Super Special #3	$2.95

Available wherever you buy books, or use this order form.

Scholastic Inc., P.O. Box 7502, 2931 E. McCarty Street, Jefferson City, MO 65102

Please send me the books I have checked above. I am enclosing $_____ (please add $2.00 to cover shipping and handling). Send check or money order - no cash or C.O.Ds please.

Name_____

Address_____

City_____State/Zip_____

Please allow four to six weeks for delivery. Offer good in U.S.A. only. Sorry, mail orders are not available to residents to Canada. Prices subject to change.   BLS591